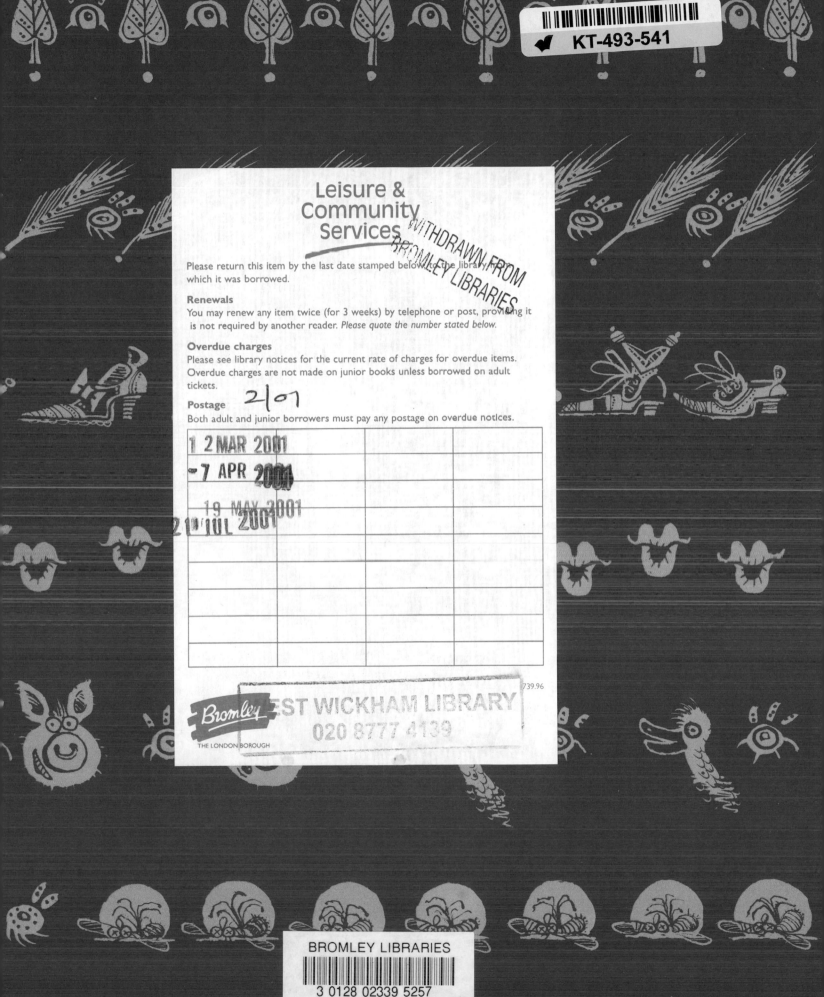

FUNKY TALES

For Martin, with love ~ V.F.

For Sally Scott and all the children and staff at
the International School of Tanganyika ~ K.P.

HAMISH HAMILTON LTD

Published by the Penguin Group
Penguin Books Ltd, 27 Wrights Lane, London W8 5TZ, England
Penguin Putnam Inc., 375 Hudson Street, New York, New York 10014, USA
Penguin Books Australia Ltd, Ringwood, Victoria, Australia
Penguin Books Canada Ltd, 10 Alcorn Avenue, Toronto, Ontario, Canada M4V 3B2
Penguin Books (NZ) Ltd, Private Bag 102902, NSMC, Auckland, New Zealand

On the World Wide Web at: www.penguin.com

Penguin Books Ltd, Registered Offices: Harmondsworth, Middlesex, England

First published 2000
1 3 5 7 9 10 8 6 4 2

Text copyright © Vivian French, 2000
Illustrations copyright © Korky Paul, 2000
All rights reserved

The moral right of the author and illustrator has been asserted

Set in Garamond 3

Printed at Oriental Press, Dubai, U.A.E

British Library Cataloguing in Publication Data
A CIP catalogue record for this book is available from the British Library

ISBN 0–241–14050–1

FUNKY TALES

Retold by Vivian French
Illustrated by Korky Paul

Hamish Hamilton • London

Another book by Vivian French and Korky Paul

Aesop's Funky Fables

CONTENTS

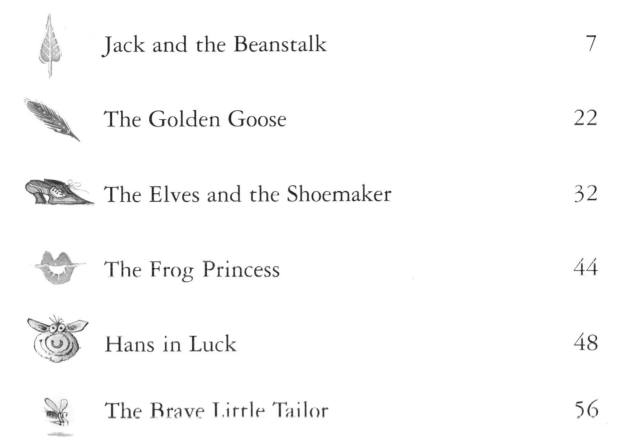

JACK AND THE BEANSTALK

Jack! Jack!
Go to market
Sell the cow –
Keep the money
Safely now.
Don't be foolish –
Come straight back –
I'll be waiting!
Hurry, Jack!

Heigh-ho.
Give a whistle, kick a pebble,
Hop here, skip there . . .
Come on, Daisy!
Heigh-ho.
Kick a pebble, give a whistle,
Skip here, hop there . . .
Come on, Daisy . . . Daisy, LOOK!
There's a funny little man and he's coming this way
And he wants to buy a cow and he says he's going to pay

With BEANS!
MAGIC BEANS!
Wah-hey!
My lucky day!!!

WHAT???
Magic beans
For my poor cow?
HOWEVER will we
Manage now?
You must have FEATHERS
In your head . . .
You NAUGHTY boy!
Go STRAIGHT to bed!!!

Sent to bed.
Beans gone.
Thrown away.
Every one.
BUT . . .

Pushing
    twisting
   thrusting
  stretching
   twirling
    whirling
   greenly
  growing
   up
    up
   up . . .
BEANSTALK!

COCK-A-DOODLE-DOO!!!

Yawn . . . yawn . . .
Have a stretch . . .
Rub my eyes . . .
SURPRISE!!!

9

There's a beanstalk at my window
    And it's stretching to the skies!
Quick!
    Open the window and
        Climb and
        Climb and
    Heave and
        Haul and
    Pant and
        Pull and –
            SLI . . .
            P P P
        And GRAB
            And pull
        And pant
            And puff and
                UP and
                    UP and
                UP
    I go . . .

I'm so high in the sky
That the clouds are far below!

WOW!

Here I am – but where is it???
That's a castle over there –
What a place – bet there's treasure –
If there's danger I don't care!
Wah-hey!!!
I'm on my way!

OH ME!
OH MY!
HERE I SWEEP
HERE I COOK
IN MY CASTLE
IN THE SKY
POLISH CLEAN –
SWEEP THE FLOOR –
EVERY DAY IS JUST THE SAME –

KNOCK! KNOCK!

THAT'S THE DOOR!
DEARIE ME!
RUN AWAY, LITTLE BOY,
RUN! RUN!
OR MY HUSBAND, THE GIANT,
WILL EAT YOU
FOR HIS TEA!

11

Please – I'm hungry!
  (HE'S SO SWEET!)
Can't you give me
Bread and meat?
I'm so tired
  (HE'S SO THIN)
  VERY WELL THEN –
  COME ON IN …

Sitting on a matchbox
Happy as can be
Thimble for my water
Happy, happy me!

What's that?
There's a rumbling mumbling
Shaking clattering
Thumping bumping stumping –
It's a GIANT!!!

  HIDE, LITTLE BOY –
  HURRY! HIDE!
  HERE'S A CUPBOARD!
  CLIMB INSIDE!

FEE FI FO FUM!!!
I SMELL THE BLOOD
OF AN ENGLISHMAN!!!
BE HE ALIVE OR BE HE DEAD
I'LL GRIND HIS BONES
TO MAKE MY BREAD!!!

Will he see me? Will he eat me?
No – his wife says he's wrong.
She says, 'Come and eat your dinner,
Cos your dinner makes you strong.'

Now he's eaten all his dinner
And he's going to have a rest –
But he's calling for his chest –
Look at that!
A bag of gold!
And a hen that can lay golden eggs!
And a harp that can sing like an angel!
HEY!
If I took the gold for my mother,
She would say
"CLEVER JACK!
WELCOME BACK!"

13

Sh . . . sh.
Is the giant fast asleep?
Sh . . . sh.
Slowly creep
And climb
And climb
And GRAB!
Then tiptoe . . .
Carefully . . .
One step more . . .
Slide to the floor
And RUN!
Back to the beanstalk
Down and
　　　Down and
　　　　　Down and
　　Down
I slither and slide . . .

Hello, Mother!
Look at me!
It's Jack!
I've come back!
Here's a big bag of gold so we're rich –
And what's for tea?

Heigh-ho.
Give a whistle, kick a pebble
Hop here, skip there . . .
Heigh-ho.
'There's nothing much to do
And there's nothing much to see . . .
At the top of the beanstalk is a beautiful hen
And I think that it's time
That the hen belonged to me!
Climb and climb
Here I go
Up the beanstalk
Once again.
I'll be back though
With that hen!

KNOCK! KNOCK! KNOCK!

Let me in –
What???
Me the boy who stole the gold?
Me the boy who came before
Knock knock knocking on your door?
Never! Not me!
All I want is a drink –
Can't you see he wasn't me?

15

Sitting on a matchbox
Happy as can be
Thimble for my water –

What's that?
There's a rumbling mumbling
Shaking clattering
Thumping bumping stumping –
It's the giant!!!

FEE FI FO FUM!!!
I SMELL THE BLOOD
OF AN ENGLISHMAN!!!
BE HE ALIVE OR BE HE DEAD
I'LL GRIND HIS BONES
TO MAKE MY BREAD!!!

No – he's eating up his dinner
Just the way he did before
All I have to do is wait –
Wait until he starts to snore . . .

Sh . . . sh!
Slowly creep
Now the giant's fast asleep . . .
Climb the table
Grab the hen –
Carefully . . .
Slide to the floor
And then –

BACK to the beanstalk
Down and
    Down and
        Down and
    Down
I slither
    and slide . . .

Hello, Mother!
Yes, I'm back!
Here's a hen.
It lays eggs all of gold, so
We'll NEVER be poor
Again.

Heigh-ho.
Kick a pebble, give a whistle,
Skip here, hop there . . .
Heigh-ho.
There's nothing much to do
And there's nothing much to see.
At the top of the beanstalk is a beautiful harp
And I think that it's time
That the harp belonged to me!
Here I go
Up the beanstalk
Once again.
I'll be back –
Clever Jack!

KNOCK! KNOCK! KNOCK!

Let me in – What???
Me the boy who stole the gold?
Me the boy who stole the hen?
Me the boy who came before
Knock knock knocking on your door?
Never! Not me!
All I want is a drink –
Just a sip, just a taste –
Can't you see he wasn't me?

18

Sitting on a matchbox
Happy as can be –

What's that?
There's a rumbling mumbling
Shaking clattering
Thumping bumping stumping –
It's the giant!!!

FEE FI FO FUM!!!
I SMELL THE BLOOD
OF AN ENGLISHMAN!!!
BE HE ALIVE OR BE HE DEAD
I'LL GRIND HIS BONES
TO MAKE MY BREAD!!!

Look! He's eating up his dinner
Just the way he did before
All I have to do is wait –
Wait until he starts to snore . . .

19

Sh . . . sh!
Slowly creep
Now the giant's fast asleep . . .
Climb the table
Grab the harp —

Master! Master!
There's a thief!

WHAT?????

Oh no! Run run RUN!
There's a crashing and a smashing
And a shaking and a quaking
And I'm panting and I'm puffing
And my heart is beating madly
And I'm getting near the beanstalk
And I'm grabbing it and sliding
Slipping slithering and sliding —
And the giant's right behind me
And he's growling and he's huffing —

MOTHER! MOTHER! BRING THE AXE!!!
ONE! TWO! THREE!

CRASH!!!!!

Hello, Mother!
Yes, it's Jack.
And I've brought you a harp
A harp that can sing –
And, Mother –
I've been thinking that a beanstalk
Is an awful lot of bother
So I'm back.

Heigh-ho!
Give a whistle, kick a pebble,
Hop here, skip there . . .

21

THE GOLDEN GOOSE

There
Were
Once
Two brothers who were tall,
Very handsome, very proud.
And
There
Was
Another little brother who was not.
They
Were
Working in the woods one day
When a teeny tiny man jumped up up up
"Give me water!
Give me bread!"
That's what he said –
"Give me bread!"

"Not me!"
"Not me!"
Said the two tall brothers
Two tall brothers, proud and handsome
"I've got cake!"
"I've got wine!"
That's what they said –
"The food is mine!"
Off they swaggered
Through the trees
Into a swarm
Of angry bees.

Then the
Brother who was small, very plain, very kind
Said
"I've got water!
I've got bread!"
That's what he said –
"I'll give you bread."

Then the teeny tiny man hopped down down down.
"Thank you, boy! Now close your eyes –"
That's what he said!
"And here's a prize."

And
There
Was
A
Golden glittering gleaming goose!
Sitting in the tree roots
Sitting, squawking
"SQUAWK! SQUAWK! SQUAWK!"

The little brother stopped.
And he stared.
Then he picked up the goose and ran ran ran.
He ran past the inn and the innkeeper's daughters
Three pretty daughters, stitching, sewing
Called out "Where do you think you're going?
Give us a feather
A golden feather
A glittering gleaming
Feather from your goose!"

So
The
Brother who was small, very plain, very kind
Stopped.
And daughter number one
Daughter number two
Daughter number three
Each took hold of a golden feather
A glittering
Gleaming
Golden feather –
AND
They were STUCK!
Stuck like glue.
Nothing they could do.
So
The
Brother who was small, very plain, very kind
Picked up the goose and he ran ran ran
And the innkeeper's daughters all ran too
Nothing they could do
Stuck like glue.

Then

A

Tall thin parson passing by

Said

"Never never never have I ever ever ever

Seen three pretty girls chase one young man!

Run away home as fast as you can!"

And he put out a hand to catch at a dress

And YES!

He was stuck!

Stuck like glue.

Nothing he could do.

And

The

Brother who was small, very plain, very kind

Went on running, running, running

And the innkeeper's daughters

And the tall thin parson

All ran too.

Nothing they could do.

Stuck like glue.

Then
A
Little washerwoman with a washing line of washing
Said
"Never never never have I ever ever ever
Seen a parson chasing three pretty girls
He shouldn't be running after ribbons and curls!"
And she put out her hand to catch at his sleeve
And she couldn't BELIEVE
She was stuck.
Stuck like glue.
Nothing she could do.

And
The
Brother who was small, very plain, very kind
Went on running, running, running
And the innkeeper's daughters
And the tall thin parson
And the little washerwoman
With her washing line of washing
All ran too.
Nothing they could do.
Stuck like glue.

Then
TOOT TOOT TOOT TOOT
TOOTLE TOOTLE TOOT!
Six tall trumpeters tootling trumpets
Four white horses dancing, prancing
Two smart soldiers marching, marching –
And the king and his daughter
In a high-wheeled carriage.
One kingly king
One sad daughter.
Never never never did she ever ever ever
Laugh or smile.
She never was glad
That's what she wasn't –
She was ALWAYS sad.

"WELL!" said the king.
"LOOK AT THAT!"
And his daughter looked
And she stared
And she nodded
And she grinned
And she giggled
And she LAUGHED!!!
GIGGLE GIGGLE GIGGLE GIGGLE
TEE HEE HEE!
"That little brother is the man for me!"

29

So
The
Brother who was small, very plain, very kind
Was married to the princess
Happily, happily.
Bells rang,
DING A DONG! DING A DONG! DING A DONG!

Then
The
Brother who was small, very plain, very kind
And the kingly king and his laughing daughter
Walked away to be happy ever after . . .

And
The
Golden glittering gleaming goose
Said
      "SQUAWK!"
She flapped her wings and she ran ran ran
And
The
Innkeeper's daughters and the tall thin parson
And the little washerwoman
With her washing line of washing
Two smart soldiers marching, marching
Four white horses dancing, prancing
And the six tall trumpeters tootling trumpets
All ran too . . .
Nothing they could do!
STUCK LIKE GLUE!

THE ELVES AND THE SHOEMAKER

Down by the sea
Was a little old town
In the little old town
Was a little old street
In the little old street
Was a little old shop
In the little old shop

Was a little old man and his little old wife –
And a little little little little LITTLE piece of leather.

"It's all we've got," said the little old man
"No one comes to buy slippers or shoes
No one comes to buy clogs or boots
I haven't got a penny. You haven't got a penny.
We haven't got a penny. There's nothing left to spend.
I'll make my very last pair of shoes.
There's nothing else to do. Our life is at an end."

So the little old man took the little piece of leather
And he snipped and he snipped
And he snipped and he snipped
And he laid out the pieces with his needles and thread
"I'm tired, little wife. I'll make them in the morning."
Then he stretched and he sighed and he went to bed.

33

When the morning came the little old man
Went slowly, slowly, down the stairs
Into his shop – and GOODNESS ME!!!
There was a BEAUTIFUL pair of shoes!
"Wife! Little wife!" And his wife came running –
"See the tiny stitches in these pretty little shoes!
Pretty little shoes for pretty little feet!
Who could have made them?
Who could have stitched them?
Put them in the window! The window by the street!"

TAP! TAP! TAP! TAP! Somebody was knocking.
Somebody was knocking at the little old door.
"May I buy those shoes? Those pretty little slippers?
I'll give you a piece of gold – or more!"

Then the little old man bought another piece of leather
Enough for two more pairs of shoes
And he snipped and he snipped
And he snipped and he snipped
And he laid out the pieces with his needles and thread.
"I'm tired, little wife. I'll make them in the morning.
Shall we hurry out and buy a little loaf of bread?"

When the morning came the little old man
Went steadily, steadily, down the stairs
Into his shop – and WELL I NEVER!
There were TWO shiny pairs of shoes!
"Wife! Little wife!" And his wife came running –
"See the tiny stitches in these shiny leather shoes!
Who could have made them?
Who could have stitched them?
Put them in the window! The window by the street!"

BANG! BANG! BANG! BANG! Someone was knocking.
Someone was knocking at the little old door.
"We want to buy those shoes – those shiny leather shoes –
We'll give you a purse of gold – or more!"

Then the little old man bought another piece of leather
Enough for four fine pairs of boots
And he snipped and he snipped
And he snipped and he snipped
And he laid out the pieces with his needle and thread.
"There, little wife. I'll make them in the morning.
Let's go and buy a little cheese as well as bread!"

When the morning came the little old man
Went skipping, hopping, jumping down the stairs
Into his shop – and JUMPING JEHOSOPHAT!
There were four fine pairs of boots!
And before the boots were even in the window
Four fine men came knocking on the door.
"Have you any boots? We want to buy them –
We'll give you a bag of gold – or more!"

The little old man and the little old woman
Grew quite rich, and they grew quite fat.
All the world came hurrying, scurrying
Clomping, stomping, pittering, pattering
They all came knocking at the little old door.
Big shoes, little shoes, slipper slopper slippers
Shoes for dancers, shoes for prancers
Stitched at night with teeny tiny stitches –
More and more and more and more.

38

The little old wife sat up one evening
"Little old husband, I've been thinking
Someone is bringing us fame and fortune.
Shouldn't we find them? Shouldn't we thank them?
Shouldn't we wait and watch and listen –
Why don't we wait tonight and see?"
And the little old man said, "I agree!"

The little old man and the little old woman
Tiptoed, tiptoed down the stairs
Down to the shop in the moonlit shadows.
There on the table was the cut out leather
There were the needles and the thread all waiting.
Tiptoe, tiptoe, hide behind the chairs . . .

Skippetty hoppitty
Pittery pattery
Two little elves
In rags and tatters
Running and tumbling
Leaped on the table
Sat themselves down.
Needles flying
Flashes of silver

Sewing thread twisting
Spinning and turning
Tipping and tapping
Of nails into leather
Tying of laces
And buttons and bows
And just as the sun
Was beginning the day
They were off and away.

The little old man and the little old woman
Looked at each other and they smiled and they nodded.
"Poor little things with their clothes in tatters!
Couldn't we make them a coat and trousers?
Cosy little shirts and a little pair of stockings?
Tiny leather shoes for their frozen little toes?"
So they sat and they stitched and they sewed and they knitted
And at last they had finished – clothes and shoes.

The little old man and the little old woman
Laid out the clothes on the table in the shop
And they hid once again, and they watched and they waited –

41

Pittery! Pattery!
Pittery! Pattery!
Skippetty! Hoppitty!
Skippetty
STOP!!!

Two little elves
Standing, staring –
Clapping, laughing,
Whistling, singing,
Tumbling into trousers
Pulling on stockings
Shrugging on shirts
Tugging on shoes –
"Aren't we the finest
Dandiest, spandiest?
Time to be going –
Time to play!"
Then off they leaped.
Off and away.

42

The little old man and the little old woman
Never ever ever saw the elves again
But they never needed luck
And they never needed money
They were happy
As happy
As happy could be
In the little old shop
In the little old street
In the little old town . . .

The little old town
By the sea . . .

43

THE FROG PRINCESS

Once there was a princess
(Pretty)
Sitting by a well
(Darkly deep)
Playing with a ball
(Bouncy bouncy)
Bouncy bouncy bouncy bouncy – SPLASH!

Up jumped the princess
(Crying)
Peeped in the well
(Darkly deep)
"Where is my ball?"
(Bouncy bouncy)
Sat down and cried and cried and cried.

THE FROG PRINCESS

Up jumped a frog
(Hippy hoppy)
Out of the well
(Darkly deep)
"I'll fetch your ball"
(Bouncy bouncy)
"Promise that you'll pay me with a kiss."

"Please!" said the princess
(Smiling)
"Jump into the well"
(Darkly deep)
"Fetch me my ball!"
(Bouncy bouncy)
"I'll kiss you when the ball is by my side."

Off went the frog
(Hippy hoppy)
Into the well
(Darkly deep)
Brought out the ball
(Bouncy bouncy)
"Give me a kiss – or three or four!"

"YUCK!" cried the princess
(Frowning)
"I won't kiss a slippy slimey frog!"
She picked up her ball
(Bouncy bouncy)
And ran and ran and ran and ran and ran.

Up leaped the frog
(Hippy hoppy)
Away from the well
(Darkly deep)
Followed the princess
(Pretty)
Until he reached the palace door.

BANG! BANG! BANG! On the knocker
"Hey!" said the king. "Who's that?"
"Only a frog," frowned the princess.
"A frog?" said the king. "Let him in!"

In came the frog
(Hippy hoppy)
Bowed to the king
("How d'you do?")
Bowed to the princess
(Politely)
"You promised that you'd pay me with a kiss!"

"NO!" stamped the princess
(Scowling)
"Go back to your well!"
(Darkly deep)
"WAIT!" said the king
(Rather firmly)
"WHAT IS THE MEANING OF ALL THIS?"

"Oh," said the princess, sighing,
"A promise is a promise – I suppose –"
She picked up the frog with a shudder
And kissed him – very quickly – on his nose.

GONE was the frog
(Hippy hoppy)
THERE was a prince
(Very fine)
Knelt to the princess
(Smiling)
"Please say you promise to be mine!"

HANS IN LUCK

Once upon a time there was a boy called Hans
And he worked and he worked and he worked and he
WORKED
For one two three four five six seven
One two three four five six seven
One two three four five six seven
Long
   Long
      Years.
And his master said
"Well done, Hans! You're a good young fellow!
Not very clever, but a good young fellow –
Now, there's wages due, of course –
I'm going to give you a fine big horse!"

Hans smiled.

He smiled and he smiled and he smiled and he smiled

"Thank 'ee, sir, that's what I wanted

Truly, sir, just what I wanted.

A horse to ride on, gallop and trot –

I'm off to see my mother and to show her what I've got!"

Off went Hans and his horse along the road

Harness jingling, jingle, jangle,

Hooves clip clopping, clip clip clopping.

Hans was whistling, Hans was singing

"I'm so lucky – I'm so clever –

A fine big horse is the best thing ever!"

Then

Hans saw a man with a black and white cow.

"Hey there, boy! That's a great big horse!

Great big appetite, great big shoes –

That's going to cost you a penny or two!"

So

Hans scratched his head.

And he thought and he thought and he thought.

"A black and white cow will bring me milk

Milk will make me butter and cheese –

I'll swap my horse for your cow, if you please!"

Off went Hans and his cow along the road

Cow's tail swishing, swish swish swishing

Cow's ears twitching, twitch twitch twitching.

"I'm so lucky – I'm so clever –

A black and white cow is the best thing ever!"

Then
Hans saw a woman with a fat pink pig.
"Goodness, boy! A black and white cow!
She'll be needing straw and hay
Let alone milking every day!"
So
Hans scratched his head.
And he thought and he thought and he thought.
"Pigs mean bacon, chitterlings, ham
There's nothing nicer than pork and peas
I'll swap my cow for your pig, if you please!"

Off went Hans and his pig along the road
Pink pig grunting, grunt grunt grunting,
Trotters pattering, pit pat pattering.
Hans was whistling, Hans was singing
"I'm so lucky – I'm so clever –
A fat pink pig is the best thing ever!"
Then
Hans saw a boy with a glossy white goose.
"Morning, Hans! That's a fat pink pig!
Parson's missing a pig like that –
A pig that's pink and a pig that's fat!"

So

Hans scratched his head.

And he thought and he thought and he thought.

"They'll think it was me that stole that pig!

They'll put me into prison and they'll throw away the keys –

A goose will make me a soft feather bed

I'll swap my pig for your goose – if you please!"

Off went Hans and his goose along the road

White goose waddling, flip flap waddling

White goose hissing, hiss hiss hissing.

Hans was whistling, Hans was singing

"I'm so lucky – I'm so clever –

A glossy white goose is the best thing ever!"

Then

Hans saw a man who was sitting on a stone.

"Well now, Hans – you're nearly home!

But look at that goose! What a skinny old bird!

No good at all, you take my word!"

So

Hans scratched his head.

And he thought and he thought and he thought.

"A stone can sharpen scissors and knives

I can earn my living with the greatest of ease –

I'll swap my goose for your stone, if you please!"

Off went Hans and his stone along the road
But the stone was heavy
          Heavy
               HEAVY . . .

So Hans sat down by the river for a rest.
He dropped the stone on the path with a crash
And it rolled into the river with a mighty SPLASH!!!

Off went Hans with a leap along the road
Hans was whistling, Hans was singing
"I'm so LUCKY – I'm so CLEVER –
A heart that's happy is the best thing ever!"

THE BRAVE LITTLE TAILOR

There was once a little tailor
And he stitched and he sewed
And he sewed and he stitched
All day, every day, weekdays, Sundays,
Holidays, jolly days, work days, fun days . . .
Until one day a fly came buzzing
Buzz buzz buzz buzz buzz buzzing
Buzz buzz buzzing round his pot of jam.

"Be off with you!" said the little tailor.

    Buzz buzz buzz.

"Fly away!" said the little tailor.

    Buzz buzz buzz.

"SHOO SHOO!" said the little tailor. "BUZZ OFF!"

But another fly came.

    And another and another

        And another and another and another –

            WHACK!!!

        Went the little tailor –

And there they were.

One two three four five six seven
Seven dead flies.

"Goodness me!" said the little tailor.
"SEVEN AT ONE BLOW!
What a champion I am!"
So he made himself a belt
And he stitched and he sewed
And he sewed and he stitched
                    "SEVEN AT ONE BLOW!"
In big big big big big big BIG letters.
Then he put down his needle and said
"No more needles and pins for me
No more tailoring! Here I go!
There's a whole big world out there to see –
I killed SEVEN with just ONE blow!"
Then the brave little tailor put on his belt
And he marched away up hills, down hills, up hills –
And wherever he went people stared.

"There's the champion! See him go!
He killed SEVEN with just ONE blow!"
And they pointed and whispered and told their neighbours
And their neighbours told their neighbours
And their neighbours told their neighbours
    Until at last
        Somebody told the king.

"What's that? What's that?" said the king.
"Seven at one blow? SEND HIM TO ME!"
So the brave little tailor marched up the road
And up the road and up the road
All the way to the palace. And the king said
"I've just the job for a chap like you
We've had a spot of bother with a giant or two
Pop along and knock 'em down and tidy them away
And seven sacks of gold will be yours today."

59

"I can do that!" said the brave little tailor, and he marched
Down the road and down the road and down the road
All the way to the woods, where he heard
            "CRUNCH CRUNCH CRUNCH!!!
            MUNCH MUNCH MUNCH!!!"
He peeped and he peered and he peeked between the trees
And he saw

            Two HUGE giants
Sitting and spitting and gobbling and slobbering and
Slurping and burping and ripping and tearing and munching
And crunching
            Meat and bones.

"Hm," said the brave little tailor.

He tiptoed here and he tiptoed there
And he filled his pockets with stones.
Then he climbed and he climbed and he climbed
To the very top of a tree. . .
    And he waited
        And he waited.
            And he waited . . .

Until at last the giants slept and snored and
Snuffled and grunted beneath him.

The brave little tailor listened.
And he looked.
And he smiled.
He pulled a stone from his pocket
And dropped it,
        PLOP!
On to the head of the giant with a beard.

UP jumped the giant with a beard and he stared
And he glared all around.
All he could see was the giant with one eye,
Sleeping and snoring and snuffling and grunting.

"OI!" said the giant with a beard. "YOU HIT ME!"
"ME?" said the one-eyed giant with a yawn.
"I NEVER EVER DID!"
"YOU MUST HAVE!" said the giant with a beard.
"AND DON'T DO IT AGAIN!"
And they slept and snored and snuffled
And grunted some more.

The brave little tailor pulled a stone from his pocket.
PLOP!
On to the head of the one-eyed giant.
UP jumped the one-eyed giant and he stared
and he glared all around.
All he could see was the giant with a beard, sleeping and
snoring and snuffling and grunting.

"OI!" said the one-eyed giant with a beard.
"YOU HIT ME!"
"ME?" said the giant with a beard with a yawn.
"I NEVER EVER DID!"
"YOU MUST HAVE!" said the one-eyed giant.
"AND DON'T DO IT AGAIN!"

And they slept and snored and snuffled
And grunted some more.

PLOP! PLOP! PLOP! PLOP!

"THAT'S ENOUGH!" roared the giants, and they leaped
to their feet.
"I'LL BIP YOU AND I'LL BOP YOU!"
"I'LL SMASH YOU TO PIECES!"
Then they bipped and they bopped
And they smashed and they bashed
Until nothing was left . . .
Except

A GREAT BIG HOLE.

The brave little tailor slid down his tree.
"I'll run to the palace to collect my gold
Then it's off and away back home for me –"

And that's the end. The story's told!

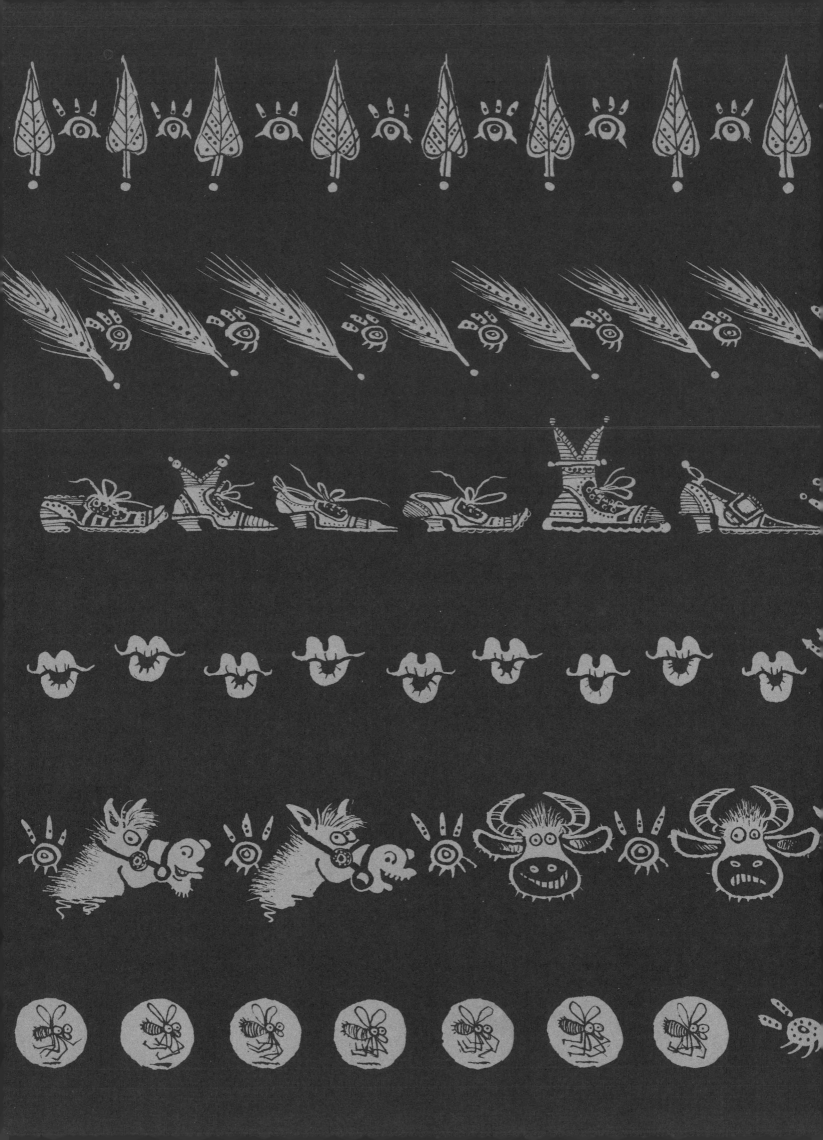